Tal and the Magic Barruget

Tal
and the Magic
Barruget

by

EVA-LIS WUORIO

illustrated by

BETTINA

The World Publishing Company

Cleveland and New York

For my friend, John Moore

Published by The World Publishing Company
2231 West 110th Street, Cleveland 2, Ohio

Published simultaneously in Canada by
Nelson, Foster & Scott Ltd.

Library of Congress Catalog Card Number: 65-19719

2 CPIHC 266

THERE WAS ONCE a small boy called Tal. He was eight
years old and he lived with his father on a small island called
Ibiza. It was in the Mediterranean Sea, and the sun shone
there most of the time.

Although he had been born in New York, he had lived in
Ibiza since he was four years old, so he hardly remembered
anything else. His mother, who had been born in Canada,
had died when he was three, so he hardly remembered her
either. His father, who had been born in Wales, which was
the reason he was named Talfryn, had always been with him,
so he naturally knew him the best.

5

Then there was the *Bruja Vieja*. That means Witch Old if
you translate it directly from Spanish, but of course if you
really put it into English it's the Old Witch. That's what the
people in the village called the old woman who looked after
Tal and his father and their small house.

They called her that quite affectionately, not as a nasty
name, because she was so old that her face was completely

6

lined. You could have played tic-tac-toe in her wrinkles. She was small and wizened too, and wore about six black skirts, all of them down to her toes, a shawl around her shoulders, and a scarf with fringe on her head. She was very kindly and very quick, and because she spoke Ibizenco, which is a dialect mixed up from Spanish and all the other Mediterranean languages, Tal spoke it too. Tal was very fond of her.

One day Tal's father said to him, "These paintings aren't selling very well. I guess I have to take to the old camera."

Tal's father painted rather strange paintings with only colors, not with people or orchards or cows or anything. Sometimes someone in London or Paris or New York bought one, and then they were very well off. Sometimes, for a long time, no one bought a single painting. That was when Tal's father usually said, "I must make a trip with my old camera." Then he'd go and film something in India or Liechtenstein or Biskra or Lapland, and sell whatever he filmed to the television people, and they had money again.

Tal hadn't really minded, when he was quite small. Bruja Vieja had taken good care of him while his father was away, and so had everyone else in the village. This was in the days before a lot of foreigners came to live there. It isn't quite the same now.

But now that he was eight years old, he really liked very much having his father around. They'd go fishing all night on a fishing boat with one little light hung over the stern. They'd go on their bicycles to the pine woods or to a far *cala* —*cala* means a bay—and have picnics and happy times. They'd go and look at pictures in the little stone galleries in the old town of Ibiza. They were very busy together. So he

7

didn't at all like the idea of his father's going away again.

"May I come too?" he asked.

"No, I think not, Tal" his father said. "You see, I'm not only thinking of making a film, but I think I'll bring back a mother for you, too."

"My mother's dead," said Tal, "and in heaven. Looking after us."

"Quite true," said his father. "But I think she would like to have a sort of a deputy here too. A nice one, that is."

"Do you know of one?" Tal asked.

"Yes I do, Tal," his father said. "That's why I think I should go and make that film, and afterwards bring her back with me."

"Will she mess up our lives?" Tal asked.

"*Hombre!*" Tal's father said. That means "Man!" and is the sort of exclamation Spaniards say on any occasion when an exclamation (!) is needed. "Certainly not. I told you she was all right."

Then he pulled at his red beard.

"Of course," he said, "I'll have to shave this beard off because she doesn't like it. And you can't go throwing your clothes around all the time, the way you do. Women don't think that's civilized. And you'll probably have to wash oftener on the days when it's not warm enough for swimming. And Bruja Vieja just will have to stop making that old rice all the time and give us some green vegetables. Women like people to eat green vegetables."

"Do we *need* her, Father?" Tal asked.

"Well, yes," said his father. "We do. You see, that's the way it is."

8

"When are you going, then?"

"Well, I thought I'd go tomorrow. Get it over and done with, see."

"When will you come back, Father?"

"As soon as I can, Tal. You'll be all right, won't you? Look after the house and think of the things I told you about."

"What things?"

"Well, you know—not throwing your clothes all about, and changing your shirt at least every day, and washing, if you haven't been swimming, and green vegetables, and weeding the garden. That sort of thing."

"You really want to do this, do you?" Tal asked.

"Yes, I do," Tal's father said.

"All right then," Tal said. "That's that, isn't it."

Chapter Two

AFTER TAL had seen his father to the bus the following morning, he climbed back home. His house was on a pine-clad hill above the village. It was low and whitewashed, with a long terrace made of old olive-tree trunks and bamboo shoots, and when the grapes ripened they could just pick bunches right there. White and purple and muscatel they were, and very good too.

The leaves on the vines were still only pale green and small, because this was in the early spring. Tal sat down in the dappled shade under them. He looked out over the fields and a couple of little white-painted farm buildings to the sea. The sea was turquoise and blue and purple, and very nice to look at.

Bruja Vieja swept the hall behind him, and then came with her broom onto the terrace. Her little black eyes were sharp.

"What's the matter, boy?" she asked. Actually what she said was, "*Que pasa, chico?*" but we won't go into Spanish here, since Tal understood it anyhow, and perhaps you don't.

"I just can't figure it out," Tal said.

"*Que?*" What she meant was, "What?"

"Why does Father think we need anybody else?" And then Tal told Bruja Vieja what his father had said.

"Well, well. Hmpf," she said. "About time too. Couldn't happen to a nicer young man. Hope she deserves him. *Bueno* —good then. What are we going to do about it, boy?"

"I just don't know," Tal said. "How am I going to remember about hanging up my clothes? I hate green vegetables. I like rice. And what's the point of washing when even in January, after a couple of days of cold, it'll always be warm enough

11

to swim? For my father and me, it is, at least." He added that because he'd never known Bruja Vieja to swim.

Bruja Vieja put down her broom. Her cat Gato climbed over the fence and joined them. All three of them sat there on the top step and looked out over the fields and the orchards to the sea.

There was a long silence. They were thinking.

Then Bruja Vieja said, "I've got it, Tal. Don't worry. I've thought of something."

"What is it?"

"Have I ever told you about the Barruget? Bruja Vieja asked.

"No," Tal thought carefully. "Do you know, I don't think you ever have."

"Well, now I will. He is the solution to our entire problem."

"Our problem, Bruja Vieja? I thought it was only mine?"

"Don't be so self-centered. It's mine too. What's yours is mine. What if she didn't like me?"

"Either, you mean. Yes, there's that, isn't there. Because of that old rice."

"Yes, and because I don't see why I should sweep under the beds every day."

"I don't either," Tal said. "So what's your solution?"

"The Barruget, boy, I told you."

"What's a Barruget?" Tal asked.

"The ignorance! The abysmal ignorance of the boy. Barruget *is*. Always has been, for that matter. You are a boy. A Barruget is a Barruget."

"Is he *like* anything?" Tal asked wisely.

"Well, you could say that he's like a gremlin. Or like a hob-

12

goblin. Or like a gnome. Or like a troll, dvergar, flibbertigib-
bet, leprechaun, genie, bhut, kelpie, familiar. Now, actually
he's more like a familiar than anything else. Only of course
he's a Barruget."

"I see," Tal said.

"Remember the day when I couldn't get the bucket up
from the well by the kitchen door?" Bruja Vieja asked. "Well,
I tell you, more than likely it was a Barruget, mad about
something, holding it down there."

"A Barruget's bad then?" Tal said.

"There are good ones and there are bad ones," Bruja Veija
snapped, "as there are of anything. People, for example."

"About this Barruget," Tal said. "What about him, then?
In our problem?"

"That's what I've been trying to tell you, if you'd only
listen. We'll capture one, and have him serve you."

"Serve me?"

"Yes—do your bidding, boy. Eat your green vegetables.
You can tell him from me to sweep under the beds. We'll
have no trouble with anyone when we have a Barruget doing
your bidding."

"Where'll we get one?" Tal asked.

"They say he lives in cisterns and wells—that's because he
probably came over to these islands with the Romans who
built the cisterns and wells—but that's not where you'll find
him. There's a trick to trapping him, and no mistake."

"I'm not very keen on traps," Tal said. "Not even mouse
traps. I wouldn't like to hurt him, you know."

"Nothing like that," Bruja Vieja said. "No traps involved,
have no fear of that. No, there's only one way of catching

13

him. He'll be worth having, mind you. He is extraordinarily quick, clever, efficient, and obedient. Really, he's the only solution to our problem."

"Tell me," Tal said. "Tell me all about it, then."

"I'm not going to until you've picked up all the things littering your room. Then you can go and have a swim. On your way back pick up two loaves of bread at Juan's. Also I think we'll need a piece of fish to put into the rice. Ask your friend Jaime the fisherman if he has any. I've my bits and pieces to do around the house. I'll get on with them and you get on with yours, and I'll tell you how we'll catch the Barruget when we're having supper."

Chapter Three

BRUJA VIEJA had made Tal a rice dish for supper. It had in it a few pieces of fish, a few pieces of chicken, some onions and tomatoes and sweet green peppers, and it was very good. They ate it in the kitchen where the floor was of red and white tiles, the stove stretched right across one wall with a hood over it, and the door opened into a back garden. The table was low and the chairs were small because neither Tal nor Bruja Vieja was very big. It was a friendly type of a kitchen.

"I'll tell you, boy," Bruja Vieja said when they were on their second helping, "it's not all that easy to catch a Barruget. First of all you have to have a black bottle."

"I've seen no-color bottles, and green bottles, and brown bottles, and even red bottles," Tal said, "but I don't remember ever having seen a black bottle."

"There it is," said Bruja Vieja. "We'll have to find one and it won't be easy. But we can't do anything without one."

"So when we've got one, what do we do?" Tal didn't think anything was impossible because his father often said to him, "Nothing's impossible, son; if you just put your mind to it." Which was the reason he wasn't too worried about finding a black bottle.

"Then we have to go down to Santa Eulalia del Rio. Remember that old bridge? Not the new bridge higher above, but the old bridge over the little cascade?"

"Of course I do," Tal said. "My father and I go there often to wash our hair when there's not much water in the well. You know, in the fresh water from the river. Soap doesn't lather in the salt sea."

"Yes, yes, yes," said Bruja Vieja. She didn't like to be told things she already knew. "Well, you've got the bridge firmly in your head? Now, do you remember the little vine flower that grows under the arches? Not an ordinary one. The one that's pale purple, pale pink, pale blue, pale yellow, with tiny golden furry edges to it?"

"I know," Tal said. "It only flowers for a moment, and when you pick it, it withers."

"That's the one. And there's the trick, to find it when it's flowering."

"That ought to be just about now," Tal cried. "Father and I washed our hair there only day before yesterday, and we saw it already in bud. We said we'd go back and look at it, and he was perhaps going to paint an idea from it. Only now he's gone. As you know."

"So," said Bruja Vieja. "So," she said softly, and her black cat came and arched his back on her shoulder. "That's very interesting indeed. It seems luck's looking for us."

"What do we do with the flower, Bruja Vieja?"

"We put it into the black bottle, while it's in full bloom, boy. We cork the bottle. Then, boy, in the morning, there is the Barruget. In the bottle. Ready and willing to do your bidding."

"My bidding?"

"Anything you ask it to do."

"Like pick up things after me? Comb my hair? Eat my green vegetables?"

"And more! And more! And more! That little familiar is a demon for work. He'll clean the house. He'll wash the sails of your boat. He'll clean the weeds out of the garden your father told you to hop to. He'll pick the grapes. He'll pick the figs. Oh, there's no end of things he'll do. He really is a veritable demon for work, I tell you."

Tal finished the rest of his rice. He wiped his mouth. (That would show the lady his father was bringing back home.) Then he went and gave a sharp hug to Bruja Vieja.

"Look, *cariña* [*cariña* means my love, and Tal loved that old woman], do you know where we can go to look for that black bottle?"

17

The Old Witch gave Tal a hug. They were really very fond
of one another.

"Listen, boy," she said, "there aren't many I'd be telling
this to, believe me. But I *think* I know where we might find
one. Are you ready to come to pick pine cones for winter
fires with me?"

18

Tal didn't particularly like picking pine cones. He knew they started fires very well, and made a pretty flame. But it was something that had to be done, often enough, so he didn't care for it.

"What do pine cones have to do with that old black bottle?" he asked.

"We don't want everyone to know what we are looking for, do we," Bruja Vieja said. "Are you stupid?"

"No," said Tal. "I'm not. So why pine cones?"

"Because on the Hill-of-the-church-that-fell-into-the-sea, that's where we might find the black bottle."

"I see," Tal said. "Now I see what you mean. We'll take our baskets and pretend we're picking pines cones there, because of the pines on the hill, and all the time we are really looking for that old black bottle?"

"You're right on, boy," Bruja Vieja said. "And we're off the minute I've done the dishes. Come to think of it, we're off right now. By tomorrow we might have a Barruget and he can do them."

Chapter Four

IN THE SPRING of the year, in Ibiza, the night comes late. Though it was past seven o'clock in the evening the sky was still nice shades of pale greens and yellows.

The old woman, almost as small as Tal and looking rather funny in her long black skirts and shawls and scarfs, and Tal, in his not too clean shorts and a blue shirt, took their baskets and went down to the village. They crossed the only street, which was not really like a street at all, and then followed the red earthen path by the sea. They passed Fishermen's Point where the boats were being made ready to go out to sea for night fishing. Then they started to climb the peculiar conical pine-clad hill.

Once upon a time, that's what the legend of the village says, there was a church at the very top of this hill. It was the first church on the island. No one had ever built anything before with such a straight tall white tower. It was built on top of some old Roman ruins. Everything Roman was in ruins because it was so long ago when they were around, building.

Everything but the viaducts and the memories. Memories keep.

Anyhow, the story went that this church at certain lights was reflected in the sea. It looked so beautiful that the sea fell in love with it. One day the sea rose, higher and higher, and smacked down the top of the hill. The church fell into the bottom of the sea. Sometimes, on a calm, clear day, you can still see it in the deep depths. On a May Day Sunday, every year, the whole village walks up to the top of the hill to remember this event.

Anyhow, what's important to this story is that when the church fell into the sea, a lot of crevices and caves in the hill cracked open. Inside these rocks many ancient things, hidden since the days of the Romans and even before them, were found. (This kind of finding is called archaeology.) There seemed to be no end to the discoveries; however thoroughly one lot of people searched, there was always still something new for others to find.

It was here that Bruja Vieja had said to Tal they might find a black bottle. The ancients had made many curious things, she said.

"Now we'll start filling our baskets with pine cones," said Bruja Vieja.

"And at the same time we look for the black bottle? Right?"

"Right," said Bruja Vieja.

Gulls wheeled about and the songs of the fishermen drifted up from Fishermen's Point. The evening breeze wafted about them the salty smell of the sea, and of the sun-hot pines, and the flowering shrubs. Farmers were saying "Whup, whup," to their horses turning the water wheels which made water run down the little ditches called *canalettas* into the fields and the orchards. The evening was so still they could hear all these sounds from far away.

They picked pine cones until their baskets were nearly full.

Then, looking for a little pile that had fallen into a crevice, on a rock close to the sea, Tal discovered a cave.

"*Vieja!*" he called. "I've discovered a cave."

Together, helping one another, they clambered down the rough, sloping passage. It ended in a narrow cavern, high enough for Tal to stand upright.

22

It was quite dark, although the evening light from the passage did flash reflections of the setting sun on the moist, shining ceiling.

"It looks like Aladdin's cave," said Tal.

23

"Aladdin who?" asked Bruja Vieja.

"Aladdin, the boy who went into the treasure cave, in the story, of course."

"I don't know anything about that. Help me move this seaweed. I wouldn't be surprised if there were something under it."

So they moved the seaweed. It was soggy and smelled of salt and fish. It was sort of squizzy, sticky green. Underneath, the next layer was all crisp and brown. Under that was another layer that was even drier, and yellow and flaky. Then, beneath, there was only sort of dust and flat rocks. The rocks looked as though someone, once long ago, had placed them very carefully, just so.

Tal threw away the dried starfish, and the dried octopus tentacles, and old skeletons of fish. Then he put his little dagger, the one his father had given him when he was six, between two of the stones. He gave it a good hoist. The stone moved. Together, he and Bruja Vieja lifted it off.

Underneath was a little cavity.

Inside this there were sprinklings of dried seaweed and some brown and red dust. In the middle of it all, whole and good as anything, there was a black bottle.

"See," said Tal, "there it is."

"Aha, I am a good Old Witch," said Bruja Vieja. She lifted the bottle and peered at it against the light. "I am indeed," she said. "Look, not even a crack. Good as it ever was. What did I tell you. I had a feeling there might be one left."

"One what left?"

"One black bottle—magic, boy, of course."

Carefully Tal took it.

24

It was a good big round-shaped bottle.
The mouth of the bottle wasn't very large.
"Can he get through that?" asked Tal.
"Better to ask can we get him into it," said Bruja Vieja.
"What do you mean, Old Mother?"
"You'll see, boy. Hurry, hurry. Soon the moon will be up."
Carefully they wrapped the black bottle in some of the dried yellow seaweed. Then they put it into the bottom of a basket and piled pine cones over it.
Then they went home.

Chapter Five

WHEN THEY got home Tal put the pine cones into a box in the woodshed and Bruja Vieja washed the black bottle with soap and water.

They lit a lamp because it was getting dark now, and placed the black bottle beside it, on the kitchen table. The bottle was so black you couldn't see through it, but at the same time it seemed to have a glow inside.

"A thousand years of dark nights," Bruja Vieja mumbled, "storms and tears, lost secrets, strange joys, are held within. Oh yes, boy. This is a very good bottle indeed. Doubtless it's been a Barruget bottle before. That's the way it seems to me."

Tal stared at it and he seemed to see ships and the sea, and fierce dark faces, and flying battlements, and a fortress against a lightning-lit sky, and a black horse racing.

"It's a good bottle, all right," he said. "Any old Barruget ought to like it, oughtn't he? What do they look like anyhow?"

"Hmpf," said Bruja Vieja. "Questions, always questions." Then she relented and explained. "They can look like any-

thing, clever little monsters that they are. They can make themselves small as a fly and big as an elephant. They can crack millstones and mend spider webs. They're difficult to catch, mind you, but well worth the trouble having, I tell you."

"Well, shall we get on with it?" Tal asked. "Never leave for tomorrow what you can do today."

"You rascal, you," said Bruja Vieja. Then she remembered. "Your pa said you were to be in bed at your bedtime."

"Bedtime surely depends on whether you've got the day's work done," Tal said. "I don't get to go to bed until I've picked up my things and brought in my bicycle, do I? Well, today's job's to find the Barruget, isn't it? So my bedtime's when we've found him."

"There's something in what you say," Bruja Vieja agreed.

27

"How far were the flowers out under the old bridge day before yesterday?"

"One or two were almost out," Tal said. "And the rest of them should be in blossom now. And you know they don't last once they're out. We'd better hurry."

"Very well then," said Bruja Vieja. "You go and put on your thick turtle-neck sweater. I'm not having a sick boy around whether I have a Barruget to help me or not. Night mists are damp. There's spray under the arches of the old bridge. Where are my seventh and ninth shawls? Light the lantern, boy."

Tal got ready in a hurry. He had the lantern lit and the door open for Bruja Vieja when she came back folding the ninth shawl over her stomach and tying it behind her back.

"Dim the light, dim the light, foolish boy," she said. "You don't want to let them know we're coming."

They went down the mountain through the pines and the gorse. 'Way out at sea fishing-boat lights dipped and blinked and Formentera Light winked back at them in a reassuring sort of way. The young moon was scudding with the clouds. Below, there were lighted windows in the village but above, where they went, there were just the shadowed paths and night silence.

They rounded the Puig, the hill on which the ancient fortress-church stands, and climbed up the age-worn steps of the small old town. Below them the river wound like a shiny road. When they got on the other side of the Puig they could hear the murmur of the little cascade under the old bridge. From farther out came the constant beat of the surf. The river was silent like the night.

28

They went past the almond orchards, ghost-flowered in the moonlight, and under the black deep shade of the fig trees and the vast-spreading algarroba trees. The nearer they got, the louder the little cascade sang.

Around the pool below the cascade the oleanders were in blossom, but the pink flowers now looked mysteriously purple in this no-light. Tal gave his hand to Bruja Vieja as they scrambled down the rocky path, and left it in her warm, firm, clawlike grasp. It felt friendly.

Now the tall, arched, deep-blue shadow of the high new bridge was over them. It seemed to make halls and tunnels all around. Everything seemed not only bigger, but utterly different from daytime. It was as though the night had its own house even in this familiar place.

29

They spoke in whispers.

"Where did you see the flowers, boy?"

"They're right at the bottom," Tal whispered, "growing out of a long crack in one of the pillars of the old bridge. Hanging down, sort of, like a net with a small starfish caught in it."

"When I was a young girl," Bruja Vieja rumbled, "and I'm not saying in which century that was, there were huge bushes of them. The old bridge was covered with them. I well remember one spring night like this . . . Well, hmpf, hmpf, well, where are they then?"

"The darkness makes everything different," Tal explained. "But I'm practically certain we're on the right path. Don't slip on the stones, Old Bruja, just follow me."

He didn't want to let go of her hand, but here they had to go single file, stepping gingerly on the slippery stones by the pool, to reach the foot of the pillars.

"You look after yourself, boy," Bruja Vieja snorted, "and I'll look after myself. There's the moon, there's the moon. Hurry up, now."

"Is the moon bad?"

"Better not to have all the light in the world for what we're up to. Though, to tell the truth," she added, peering at the moon over her left shoulder, "it's just right, just right for what we want."

Tal had nearly slipped, then he nearly fell, and his eyes were getting somewhat heavy, and he was beginning to worry about not finding the place at all, when he put his hand against the rough old stone of the pillar, and there it was. He'd crushed the flower and a smell that was something

like the sound of little silver bells floated to his nose. The tiny furry prickles of the flower stuck into his palm and it, too, smelled inexpressibly sweet.

"I've found it!"

"Just about time too. Where's the lantern? Stand steady, boy."

31

Bruja Vieja stuck her nose into the delicate flowers. She was nearsighted.

"They're the ones all right," she announced. "And a good thing we came tonight. They're in the prime of condition. Tomorrow they might have been gone. Ah, never did I think to see them again."

"I'll always from now on come and pick you some," Tal promised. "Every spring."

"Hmpf." Bruja Vieja became extremely busy. "Hold the lantern higher. Where's the black bottle? Did you bring a cork? That's all right, I had the foresight. A good cork it is too; been saving it for an emergency. Handy things to have, corks. Lot of people throw them out, but you never know, do you. Where would we be now, if I'd thrown the corks away, I ask you? Don't bother to answer. Can you hang the lantern from that jutting rock? Steady, boy. Now hold the bottle here, closer."

Tal held the bottle steady.

The lantern light flickered palely on the hanging flower-studded vine. Even in the faint light their delicate tracery was there to wonder at.

"Quiet," said Bruja Vieja.

Tal couldn't even hear the cascade or the surf any more.

"Click and clack," said Bruja Vieja, and with her sharp nail she cut the thin stem of the flower, bent close to Tal, popped the flower into the black bottle and, all in the same motion, corked it.

"Well," she said, and chuckled softly and long. "A good night's work if ever I saw one done."

Chapter Six

THE FISHERMEN WERE sounding the sea shell, announcing their catch, when Tal woke up the next morning. It's such a big shell you need two hands to hold it, and strong lungs to blow it. Tal loved the sound, for it is like the wind in the masts of the sailboat, with a little shout of the gulls and susshing of the seas and a big liner's hoot, all in one.

He knew it must be early because the fishermen got back soon after dawn.

For the first second awake he thought, his father wasn't at home, so why was he feeling so excited?

But yes! The black bottle!

The Barruget!

He whipped out of bed and ran outside. There, on the far end of the terrace, under the spring-pale green of the grape-vine, Bruja Vieja was doing the wash. She was in all her skirts and shawls. Sometimes Tal wondered if she ever undressed even to sleep.

"Don't wash anything more!" he shouted. "Stop right now!"

The wizened old woman grinned at him. Though she was almost toothless and her skin was crisscrossed with lines, she often looked just lovely, Tal thought.

"Have you lost your tiny wits, boy?" she asked.

"You don't have to do that any more." Tal skipped around her in his striped pajamas. "Don't you remember? Don't you remember? Don't you remember? *We've got a Barruget!*"

"Sure enough," Bruja Vieja swept the soapsuds off her forearms. "I wonder if it's taken."

"What do you mean?"

"Well, there's this and there's that to it. It's not all that simple."

"But we got the right black bottle. And the moon was just right. And the flowers were just right. Let's go and see!"

"There's just one person who can command him, boy," Bruja Vieja said warningly. "Are you able and willing?"

"I am! I am! Wait and see. Where's the bottle?"

"I put it in the pantry," said Bruja Vieja. "With the other bottles. And this and that. Hadn't you better have breakfast first?"

"No," said Tal firmly. "Now."

So they fetched the bottle, and before Bruja Vieja was able to get out another warning, Tal had whipped the cork off it.

There was a little puff like a blown dandelion bursting, and then a small green hand appeared at the mouth of the bottle. Another hand. A head. Shoulders. A little man was climbing out. He slid down the bottle and began to grow. Tal was quite tall for eight years old, but not all that big.

34

This little fellow grew until he was about up to Tal's shoulder. He had a huge head with immense ears, the biggest mouth you've ever seen, and little beady green eyes. He looked dwarfish and gnomish and hobgoblinish all at once.

While they stared at him—even Bruja Vieja looked stunned —he opened his mouth wide and bellowed, "WORK OR FOOD WORK OR FOOD WORK OR FOOD!"

"Wh-wh-what's he saying?" Tal took a step backward.

The little man wrung his hands and opened his mouth wide. "WORK OR FOOD!" he screamed.

"That's what they always say," Bruja Vieja looked at the little demon fondly. "Work or food, work or food. They don't stop bellowing until you give them one or the other. He likes a lot of it, whatever it is."

"Would you please—" but Tal couldn't make his voice heard over the bellowing.

"WORK OR FOOD WORK OR FOOD WORK OR FOOD!"

"Go and finish the wash on the terrace," Tal shouted as loudly as he could. "Rinse it well. In the canaletta by the garden gate. Hang it up."

Ppfffuuuit!

The little fellow disappeared.

"Whew," said Tal. "He certainly is noisy, isn't he."

"I've got a slab of fish for your breakfast," said Bruja Vieja.

"I hope he hasn't really disappeared," Tal said. "I'll just check."

There, sure enough, at the far end of the terrace, suds were flying in clouds, washing was getting brighter than light, and a little humming sound seemed to indicate that the Barruget was happy.

"He's at it, all right," Tal reported. "I'll have my fish, please."

He wasn't half finished with his breakfast when the little demon whipped back.

"WORK OR FOOD!" he bellowed.

"My room, clean my room, under the bed, put everything into its—" Ppfffuuuit, the little fellow was gone.

"Well," said Tal, "he's certainly fast. What'll we give him to eat?"

"He doesn't need both," said Bruja Vieja. "Just work. OR food."

"Yes, but it's his first morning," Tal said. "I think we should give him a little bit of something. After all, how do we know how long it's been since he's—" He didn't get his sentence finished.

"WORK OR FOOD!" The little demon was bouncing in front of him impatiently.

"You *couldn't* have done my room yet," Tal said. "It takes me *hours!*"

"WORK OR FOOD WORK OR FOOD WORK OR FOOD!"

"All right, then. Get on with the geranium bed, and the plot of iris at the bottom of the garden. There're the weeds, and the snails to be collected for the chickens, and the bougainvillea leaves to be swept up and—"

Ppfffuuuit. The little man was gone.

"My," said Tal, "he tires me out. What'll I do when I can't think of anything else for him to do?"

Bruja Vieja cocked her head at him. "Hmpf," she said.

"And how do I get him back into his bottle while I think?" Tal asked.

"You should have thought of that before you pulled out the cork, boy," Bruja Vieja cackled.

Chapter Seven

TAL RUSHED THROUGH the rest of his breakfast because he realized he'd be busy thinking of things for the Barruget to do later.

Oddly enough, this job seemed to take him longer, so Tal had a chance of running to his room. All his things were neatly stacked in their places. His clothes were hung up. His *alpargatas* and sandals were in a row in the cupboard. The floor was washed and the bed was made. He rather thought even the windows had been cleaned.

He looked out into the back garden and there on the line was a long string of sparklingly clean washing, drying in the morning breeze.

Tal went back to the kitchen.

"He sure is a good little worker," he reported. "As I was saying, I think we ought to give him some food. Goodness knows when he last ate."

"Could be some two thousand, seven thousand years ago," Bruja Veija muttered. "I don't recognize him myself. Must have been long before my time when he was last out."

"What'll we give him? Is there another piece of fish?"

"You don't know what you're talking about, boy. A little piece of fish, indeed," Bruja Vieja said. "Those Barrugets, they eat the way they work. Lots of both. I don't even know what we've got in the house for him, not having bought anything special as your pa's away. Let me see, there's that ten kilos of rice I got cheap after Rosita's wedding."

"Ten kilos! Why, that's over twenty-five pounds or something, isn't it. It would take a hundred people to eat it, I bet."

"Just about right for a small snack for a Barruget," said Bruja Vieja. "At least I know what I'm talking about, which is more than you do."

Grumbling to herself, she hunted out the biggest pot they had, which was pretty big because it had been left behind by the farmer who'd sold them the house, and he'd boiled huge whole pigs in it for sausages.

It was so big and heavy that Tal had to help her get it on the fire, although the fire grille was on the floor. She poured

a bottle of oil into it, and threw in a handful of garlic.

"He'll eat us out of house and home," she muttered, "and blessed if I know what your father's going to say when he gets back."

She had to put two whole pailfuls of water into it. Big pails too.

It was heavy work, and Tal said, "I'll get him to do that for you, watch if I won't."

Then she poured in bags and bags of rice, and said, "Hadn't you better start thinking how to get him back into the bottle if you can't find more jobs for him to do?"

"I've thought that maybe I'll take him down to the boat," Tal said. He and his father had a little sailboat moored off Fishermen's Point. "Father said I ought to scrub the decks and spread the sails in the sun, and Jaime was to help me. But I don't see that I need to ask Jaime now that I've got that busy Barruget around."

"How are you going to get him down there?" again Bruja Vieja chuckled. "I can see it. You and he, walking hand in hand through the village. What do you think the people will say?"

"Well," Tal said thoughtfully, "if I got him into the bottle first, see, and took him down in the bottle, see, and *then* asked him to do it, that would fix it, wouldn't it?"

"How are you going to get him into the bottle?"

Tal went over and snuggled Bruja Vieja. "You'll tell me how, that's how."

"Oh you, boy," said Bruja Vieja and rumpled his hair. "You'll be the death of me, watch and see." Then she said, "What you need is an incantation."

"A what? Please?"

"Incantation. A spell. The magic words. You ought not to meddle in these things if you know from nothing."

Tal felt it would be wiser not to point out that he hadn't been meddling in magic *alone.* So he just said, "Where do I get this in-the-cantation from?"

"He's your Barruget. You must make it up."

"How?"

"You can print, can't you? Make a verse, sort of. That's all there is to it."

"That's really all?"

"Well . . ." Reluctantly Bruja Vieja told him the important part. (She often liked to keep things to herself, and why not?) "You have to say some of it backward."

"Oh, I see," Tal said. "Very well."

At that very instant the Barruget came in like a flash.

He started bellowing immediately, "WORK OR FOOD WORK OR FOOD WORK OR FOOD!"

"Food," shouted Tal. He'd have to think fast. He would have to think up the incantation while the Barruget ate. He'd have to think pretty fast indeed because at the moment he couldn't figure out anything else for the little demon to do.

The Barruget was going through the twenty-five pounds of rice (which makes quite a lot of boiled rice, if you know that one handful is enough for two big people), and in between he was whipping into the pantry and stuffing raw potatoes, eggs in their shells, whole loaves of bread, butter and the dish it was in, into his mouth.

It was a pleasure, Tal thought between attempts to figure out the incantation, to watch that Barruget eat.

Chapter Eight

WHILE THE BARRUGET was shoveling in food like a small army, Tal ran into the garden. Not only had the Barruget cleaned and clipped the geranium hedge (geraniums grow into bushes six feet tall in Ibiza), he'd also weeded all the flower beds, swept and weeded the gravel walks, mended the fence, pruned the roses, cleaned up the morning glory that covered the little summerhouse, mended the swing and the broken garden chair, tied up the grapevine and turned the earth in Bruja Vieja's vegetable garden, all ready for another planting.

No wonder it had taken him nearly half an hour.

"I just can't think up enough things for him to do," Tal told himself. "Not that fast. I'll just have to get him back into that bottle while I think."

The first thing that came to his mind was that the Barruget wasn't very pretty. Probably he was unhappy about that. Father was always talking about the power of suggestion, Tal remembered. I'll make him *think* he's happy, Tal decided.

"*Happy* little Barruget," he said aloud.

"Why, that sounds quite nice. Now I'll put it backward."

Which he did.

"Tegurrab elttil yppah."

That sounded like an incantation all right.

He tried it out again:

> "Happy little Barruget,
>
> Well met!
>
> Tegurrab elttile yppah,
>
> Tem llew!"

That sounded fine to Tal. Why, it even sounded slightly Welsh, as when his father sang the old Welsh songs sometimes.

But surely there ought to be a little more. He thought and thought.

Suddenly a real verse popped into his head:

> "Help me in my work, and I
>
> Will give you freedom, by and by."

Now, why had he thought of that? He had no intention of losing such a useful little Barruget. Not every boy had one. And after all, it had been difficult, not to say a little scary, to get him under the old bridge at night. No, he wouldn't give him freedom. He'd think up another incantation.

But he didn't have time.

"Boy!" Bruja Vieja was shouting. "Boy, get in here! Where's your incantation? He's starting to eat the chairs now! There isn't a crumb for a small worm left in this house! Hurry!"

Tal rushed into the kitchen.

The Barruget was gnawing the leg of the kitchen chair. He stopped just long enough to bellow at Tal, "WORK OR FOOD!"

44

"Happy little Barruget,
　　　　　Well met!
Tegurrab elttil yppah,
　　　　　Tem llew!
Help me in my work, and I
Will give you freedom by and by.
Happy little Barruget,
　　　　　Tem llew!"

The Barruget stopped chewing the chair leg. He stared fiercely at Tal. His ears changed color rapidly from green to purple to puce, yellow to orange to crimson, violet back to bright green. It lasted only a second. Then he bellowed:

"WORK OR FOOD WORK OR FOOD WORK OR FOOD!"

If Tal and Bruja Vieja hadn't clapped their hands on their ears, they'd have gone deaf.

Crunch-swog! The Barruget took a mighty bite out of the corner of the kitchen table.

"It didn't work" Tal cried. "My magic's no good."

"It didn't, did it," cackled Bruja Vieja.

"What'll we do now?"

"He's your Barruget, boy. You think of something. You're responsible."

"WORK OR FOOD! WORK OR FOOD!"

"Go and chop our winter logs! All those old dry olive trees by the back gate. Into small pieces!"

Ppfffuuuit! The Barruget had gone.

"Oh dear," said Tal. "I just don't know what I'm going to do."

He dropped down cross-legged on the tile floor. He looked woebegone. Bruja Vieja had to turn her back to him. She hated to see him look miserable.

"I won't be able to think of more work for him to do unless I get a little peace," Tal said. "What was wrong with my in-can-can—you know?"

"Incantation," said Bruja Vieja smartly. "It was all right as far as it went. But it didn't go very far."

"It was all I could think of at the time," Tal said.

"You made him a promise, didn't you," Bruja Vieja looked at him shrewdly. "Why did you do that?"

"You mean all that about giving him his freedom? Well, I just happened to think of it. I thought he'd like that."

"But how does he know you are going to keep your promise? He's out of the bottle now, and I bet he intends to stay out."

"I promised, didn't I?" Tal said indignantly. "My father says a real man always keeps a promise."

"Brings to my mind an old story I once heard, that does," Bruja Vieja said slowly. "There was this boy called Pepet. An Ibizenco boy he was. And the giant of the mighty rock of Vedra—"

"WORK OR FOOD!" the Barruget was back, bouncing and screaming.

"Oh, do help me, Bruja Vieja!" Tal cried.

"All right, boy, all right. Tell him to bring in the wash and iron it, and to chop up some coal for my cooking fires."

"Iron the wash," Tal shouted. "Chop the coal!"

Ppfffuuuit! The Barruget was off.

"Dear Bruja Vieja," Tal put his arms around the old

47

woman. "If you really wanted to, you could help me, couldn't you. Please?"

"Well, now, as I was starting to tell you about this boy Pepet and the giant of the mighty rock of Vedra—"

"Please! Please tell me the story another time. Just help me with my incantation now, before that old Barruget is finished with all the work again."

"Ssshus, boy. Listen to your elders. The story is applicable to your problem. But will you listen. Well, I'll cut it short. In short, I'll cut it. It ends in an old Ibizenco saying which goes like this:

"I conte acabat
si no es mentida
es veritat."

"I see," Tal said. "It means, in proper Spanish, 'This what I've just said is no lie, it's the truth,' doesn't it?"

"More or less, boy, more or less," the old woman was obviously pleased with him. "Well, you try that on the end of your chant and see if it works."

"Do you think he understands Ibizenco?"

"Boy! What are you thinking of! Ibizenco's the oldest language spoken by the shores of our old, old sea. People so different your small mind couldn't imagine them, for thousands of years—"

"WORK OR FOOD!"

The Barruget slid to a stop in front of Tal. He began to bounce. His green feet turned violet. His eyes glittered. He was very anxious for more food, or more work. His voice kept growing louder, "WORK OR FOOD."

Tal stood up. He put his hands behind his back. He stared

48

straight into the eyes of the little monster. Then he said
clearly and loudly:

"Happy little Barruget,
Well met!
Tegurrab elttil yppah,
Tem llew!
Help me in my work, and I
Will give you freedom by and by."

He took a deep breath and said even louder:

"*I conte acabat
si no es mentida
es veritat!*

Tem llew!"

A funny rumbling sound came from the Barruget. He
stopped making his ears and feet change color. He said:

"*Bono, tu comandes,*" which means, "Fine, you give the
order."

"Into your bottle!"

Like lightning the Barruget scrambled up the leg of the kitchen table. He snatched up the black bottle. He shook it. He put it down. Then, making himself small in a flash, he scrambled in.

Bruja Vieja clamped down the cork.

"Well," she said. "*Bueno!*"

"It worked." Tal couldn't quite believe it. "Bruja Vieja, did you see, my magic worked!"

"It wasn't too bad," said Bruja Vieja. "But you certainly took your time about it. Just look at that chair!"

Chapter Nine

For the rest of that day, and most of the next, Tal was so tired from having thought up things for his Barruget to do that he didn't let him out of the bottle at all.

Probably just as well. After all, if the little man hadn't done a day's work or had a single good meal for some two thousand, or even perhaps seven thousand years, no doubt he was feeling a bit tired, too.

Anyhow, he'd done such a good job cleaning up Tal's room there was hardly anything to pick up or put away, and, as we know, the garden was spic and span.

The Bruja Vieja didn't mention the Barruget to Tal. Of course she kept glancing at him sideways, the way she always did when there was something potent on the tip of her tongue but she was keeping it to herself.

Tal was glad about that because, as he told himself, "It's my problem."

His father often said, "It's my problem." That's where Tal had got the phrase. Then, he now told himself, Father sits

down with his problem, thinks it out, makes a decision and then acts on it.

So that's what Tal did.

It was after his siesta (that helpful little midafternoon snack of sleep all sensible people take), the second day after the Barruget had been captured, that Tal outlined his plans to Bruja Vieja.

"Now," he said, "the way I see it is this. We've got two problems. We have to find work for him, and we have to find him food. Right?"

"Right," said Bruja Vieja. She stopped chopping the mushrooms they were having in their omelet for tea, and sat down to listen to Tal.

"Well," said Tal, "there's the planting of your vegetable garden, and chopping the wood for winter, and there's keeping my room clean, and there's the boat. Right?"

"Right," said Bruja Vieja.

"But the way that little fellow whips through work, that's not going to take him long. Right?"

"Go on, get on with it then," said Bruja Vieja. She was getting tired of saying "Right."

"So what I thought was this," Tal said. "I'm going to have him do a little bit of this and that in the village, see?"

"Such as what?"

"Well, old Juan the baker's got lumbago. So my Barruget could do the baking for him. It's heavy work; after all he does it for the whole village. Jaime the fisherman wants to beach his boat and caulk and paint it, and that's a big job. My Barruget can help him. Then there's the road up here to the house that gets so muddy when it rains, and the back lanes need cleaning up and graveling, and the main street needs paving, and it could use a few trees planted there too, what with the old ones they cut down when they widened it, my father says. And Antonio the cobbler wants to turn his shop into a restaurant, but he can't get any workmen cheap enough, and Creu the builder needs a few helping hands with his projects, he was telling me. Lots of things. See?"

Bruja Vieja grinned at him. "What's the village going to say about all this?"

"I'll have to see about that," Tal said. "I should think they'd be glad."

He stood up and put his hands into his pockets. He rather wondered what they were going to say too. But his father always said, if there's something you are shy about doing, do it right away, and it won't seem so bad. So he went in and fetched the black bottle, put it into his *capacho,* or basket, slung that around his neck from the long handles, the way he always did, got out his bicycle, and coasted over the bumps and cracks and cart furrows into the village. That road really did need fixing, he thought. In fact all of them did. And so did the road to Es Cana, and the one to San Carlos. . . . He began to get quite excited about his plans.

Bruja Vieja quickly wiped her hands on a piece of old newspaper, put on a few more shawls and skirts and skipped off after him. She could hardly wait to see what was going to happen. She cackled happily to herself. Why, it was like the good olden times.

Tal thought he might as well get his own boat cleaned up first.

So he bicycled down the shore path, which was just a tiny little strip of red earth between the sea and the fields and orchards, and you had to be pretty clever to keep two wheels of a bicycle on that. The black bottle in his capacho bumped against his back. He hoped it didn't make the little Barruget dizzy.

Down by the fields of maize and the fig orchards he rode, waving with his left hand to the people he knew in the fields. He could now ride his bicycle with one hand. But only with the right one.

He came to a point of tall thin firs, with shacks for the fishermen's gear and lots of fishing boats, some on shore and some in the little bay. This was Fisherman's Point.

His friend Jaime the fisherman was frying bread and to-matoes and a piece of sausage on a tiny fire. "Have some, Tal?" he called.

Coming through the pines, from the point of the old church, strolled Creu the builder.

Of all the people in the village, Jaime and Old Creu were Tal's best friends. Jaime was young and sinewy and sometimes very angry and sometimes very gay, but never unkind. Creu the builder was an old man who walked slowly, always had time for Tal, knew countless stories, and was always kind.

"Well met," said Tal. He and his Ibizenco friends spoke the Ibizenco language together because after all he'd learned it when he was very little. Sometimes the words sounded like a song.

"Well met, *chico mio*," said Creu. *Chico mio* means my boy.

55

"I have a problem," Tal said, leaning his bicycle against a tall thin pine, and ducking his head to get out of the long handles of his capacho. "May I ask for your help, *amigos?*" The old language always sounded rather formal.

"We are here to serve you," said Jaime the fisherman and Creu the builder. In English they'd probably have said, "O.K., tell us. We'll help you, whatever it is."

"Well," said Tal, "here in my basket I have a bottle, and in that bottle I have a Barruget."

Jaime dropped his chisel. After eating he was going to scrape the rust off the keel of his boat.

Creu called his dog. He always called his dog when he needed to think.

"A real Barruget," Tal said. "We caught him, Bruja Vieja and I, couple of nights ago. And my problem is to find him enough work."

They looked at him unbelievingly.

"It's a long time, a long time indeed, boy, since there have been Barrugets on the island," Creu finally said.

"Well," Tal said, "the fact was that I needed him. Shall I tell you why?"

So then he told Creu the builder and Jaime the fisherman just how his father had gone away, and what he had said before he went, and what Bruja Vieja and he, Tal, had done since.

They listened to him in silence.

"*Bueno, bueno,*" said Old Creu the builder.

"My grandmother on my mother's side," said young Jaime the fisherman, "used to tell us stories of Barrugets when we were children."

"Oh, of course," Creu said. "Barrugets are *facts*. Otherwise

56

there wouldn't be all the old stories. Everyone knows they exist. Only we have been so busy getting modern, we have forgotten to remember them."

"Shall I show you?" Tal asked.

The sea slurped among the rocks by the point and slushed softly by the fishing boats drawn near. It was a still afternoon, but even so there were curious little waves rippling on the surface. The sea likes to hear everything that's going on.

Creu the builder and Jaime the fisherman looked at one another. Then Creu said, "All right, boy. Do that."

"I'll get him to do my boat first, so you can see that he doesn't do any harm. Right?"

"Fine, boy. Truly."

So Tal took the black bottle out of his capacho, rubbed it against his stomach to make it shine, put it down between his feet and pulled the cork out.

Right away, like a mushrooming cloud, a balloon like a blown daffodil came out, and then they could see the little clawlike green hands. The Barruget hoisted himself out of the bottle.

He slid down it, stepped out to face Tal, made himself grow bigger and flapped his ears. Then his ears grew huge and his body swelled. He opened his mouth and stretched it wider and wider and wider. "WORK OR FOOD WORK OR FOOD WORK OR FOOD!" he bellowed.

Tal stood up. He put his hands behind his back. He had to smile. He found he was so pleased to see that little demon Barruget.

"Go and wash my boat. Wash the sails. Scrub the decks. Empty the bilge."

Ppfffuuuit.

The Barruget was gone.

Where Tal's and his father's boat had been swaying gently at its moorings there was suddenly a splash and a shout, spume and suds, and a happy little hum reached them.

"You see," Tal said, "he *likes* to work."

"*Bueno, bueno,*" said Old Creu. "I do remember being told . . ."

"Me too," Jaime said. "My grandmother used to say that if only we had a Barruget to do our work . . ."

"It really is true then," Tal said happily. "He has always been."

"That is certain," said Old Creu. "He has always been."

"We'll have to figure this out," said young Jaime. "Have some of my fried bread and tomato, Tal."

Just as he said that the Barruget was back with them.

"WORK OR FOOD WORK OR FOOD WORK OR FOOD!" he bellowed.

"Jaime, tell him what you want done with your boat—quickly, please," Tal shouted above the din.

"What do you mean? It's a week's job. More. It'll take three men a week with the sails and nets and all."

"WORK OR FOOD!" the Barruget stamped his foot at Tal.

"JAIME'S BOAT," Tal shouted. "Go with him Jaime, and tell him what must be done."

Jaime's face was a sight to see. He started off but the Barruget didn't follow. The little demon kept bellowing at Tal and stamping his large green feet angrily.

"WORK OR FOOD!"

"Jaime! Please tell me what you want done," Tal cried. "Quickly!"

So Jaime did, and Tal repeated it after him to the Barruget, and Ppfffuuuit, the Barruget was off.

"Whew," said Jaime. "He sure is a noisy little fellow. Do you mind if I go and see what he's done on your boat?"

"Of course not. Do," Tal said.

Old Creu looked long at the sea. Then he turned to Tal.

"You are one of the lucky ones, my boy," he said. "It isn't everyone—"

Tal never found out what he was going to say because Jaime came running back, shouting, "It's the cleanest boat I have ever seen! The sails are sparkling white! I must go and see what he is doing with mine!"

And he ran off.

"Well now, my boy," said Old Creu. "Can you control him? Can you get him back into the bottle when you want to?"

"Yes, sir," Tal said. "Indeed I can."

"Good," said Old Creu, lighting his pipe. "Then we can talk in peace about your problem of finding work for him."

59

Chapter Ten

WELL, ON THE ISLAND they still talk about what happened during those days when Tal had the Barruget, long long before any tourists came to Santa Eulalia.

It was a lucky thing that Tal happened to consult Old Creu the builder about his problem, right at the beginning.

Old Creu was a much-respected and much-liked man, and whatever he said everyone in the village accepted. Without him, Tal might have had some problems, all right. After all, not everyone remembered the olden days, or believed in the stories of Barrugets.

But because Old Creu was there to remind the villagers that Barrugets had lived on the island as long as, if not longer than any people, of course they remembered they'd heard the stories once. Anyhow, Ibizencos are very superstitious people. Superstitious nowadays means that you believe in things you can't prove. In the olden days that the Bruja Vieja was always talking about, it meant you believed that the impossible was possible and took it in your stride.

In those days people believed that there lived little green people in the forests who helped you if you were kind to them. They believed there were big friendly monsters in the sea, and that in the depths there were rainbow-colored cities and villages. They didn't have to see things to believe in them. There was magic everywhere. A lot of Ibizencos are still a bit like that.

So when Old Creu, that same night playing dominoes with his friends at Gabriel's Kiosco, mentioned that Tal had a Barruget, no one doubted him. In fact they began to reminisce about all the Barrugets they'd heard about, and the tricks they'd played, and one or two even claimed they'd seen a Barruget, once.

Tal himself had put the little Barruget into the black bottle right after he had finished cleaning and caulking Jaime's boat, because by then it was getting on to dusk, and Bruja Vieja had turned up to say it was time for tea, and bed.

In any case, as it was Old Creu who told the people in the village about Tal's Barruget, nobody got upset about this rather unusual happenstance.

When, the next morning, Tal stopped to talk to Juan the baker, to ask him if he'd like to have the Barruget help him, Old Juan merely grunted, "Delighted, boy. He can have six big loaves for his wages, and you can have two of your choice, for bringing him."

"Why, that's very kind of you," said Tal. "Thank you. I've been worried about feeding him. He has a very good appetite."

Jaime, who was walking by with his fishing nets over his shoulder, heard this and said, "Don't you worry about that,

Tal. I went out in my friend Antonio's boat this morning, and we had a good catch. If you are coming down to the Point, we'll give you lots for your Barruget."

"As a matter of fact," said Tal, "I was just on my way there. I thought you'd like to have the Barruget finish the job on your boat."

When Jaime and Tal got down to Fishermen's Point there was a great commotion going on. A huge old boat had been submerged in the bay for a couple of years. Now the owner wanted to get it on shore, dry it out, and fix it up. It looked to Tal about a hundred feet long if not more, and the bow that was touching the shore rose as high as the slender firs. There were some thirty men, fishermen and farmers and villagers, all trying to get it ashore. They were stripped to the waist, and had their trousers rolled up—not that there was much point rolling them up, because they were waist-deep in the sea anyhow, and those on shore were wet with sweat.

"Why," said Tal, slinging the handles of his capacho over his head and putting it down carefully, because of the black bottle, "my Barruget can give them a hand."

"Come and help, Jaime," the men called.

"I'll do better than that," Jaime shouted, laughing. "Stand aside, boys. Tal is going to tell his Barruget to help you!"

Everybody shouted and laughed. They were fishermen and farmers, who hadn't heard Creu the builder's story. But of course they knew what a Barruget was and they thought Jaime was joking.

Some of the ones on the close side of the big boat saw Tal uncork the bottle. They remembered the old stories, so they stopped working to stare.

The huge old craft swayed dangerously, more than half

62

full of water as it still was. Even now the water was leaking through the rotten old sides like sprays from a fountain.

The men on the other side, who couldn't see what was happening, began to shout, "Hey! What are you guys up to? Push on! Hold the boat!"

But by now the Barruget was climbing out of the bottle, and all the men who could see it dropped everything they were doing and stared.

The Barruget stretched and spread a little. Then he saw Tal, rushed up to the boy, stamped his green feet and bellowed, "WORK OR FOOD!"

"Get that boat on shore," Tal ordered. "Hold it fast until the men can secure it on the slip. Work you get, my Barruget!"

Ppfffuuuit, the Barruget was gone.

Wwhhhooossh! the big boat came on shore like a toy. The men who'd been trying to get it there all morning gasped. There it was, running up the slip like greased lightning.

"Secure the blocks!" Jaime shouted.

But before anyone could do a thing, the huge boat was firm on its stand, and *splash, crash, smash, dash,* water and seaweed and muck from the shallows, fishbones and sand and stones and jellyfish came flying over the side. The Barruget really put his shoulders to that job. *Fling, flong, flung,* the dirt sailed from the boat. *Swoosh,* the water ran out.

Everybody watched, standing as near as he could get, but out of the way of the flying debris.

It was such a really huge old boat that it took the Barruget a good hour and a half to finish cleaning it. Then he jumped over the side and came to Tal.

"WORK OR FOOD!" he bellowed.

"Go and finish Jaime's boat," Tal said. "That's what we really came here to do. Clean the keel, tar the bottom, paint the decks, patch the sails, mend the nets. I'll try to find you some food when you've—"

Ppfffuuuit, the Barruget had gone off to do his bidding.

"I'm going to cook that little guy a huge potful of fish stew," said Jaime. "He sure deserves it."

"Oh," said the other fishermen, "we'll be glad to add whatever we have left from our catch to the pot. He's certainly helpful. He eats a lot too, doesn't he, Tal?"

"Yes," said Tal, "he eats rather well."

"Well now, well now," said the owner of the big boat. "He's saved us a lot of work already, and it seems he's still doing his share. I'll tell you, Tal, there will always be a basket of fish for him from our every catch—and men," he turned to the fishermen who worked for him, "remember, every morning, to keep a choice fish for Tal and his family. A workman is worth his hire, that's what I always say."

Right then old Creu the builder came along the shore with his dog.

"Ah, there you are, Tal, boy," he said. "I was looking for you. I need a load of building material up on the hill tomorrow and my carts just can't get up that bad road. I wouldn't even *ask* my horses to try, and for my men to carry the stuff up would take days. Do you think you might tell your Barruget to help me?"

"Certainly, sir," Tal said. "And why don't we fix the road while we're about it? All he needs is the materials to do the job."

Tal had figured this out, you see, because in the garden they had tools for the work, Jaime had his paints ready on the boat, and the patches for his sails, and the line to mend his nets. Also, Juan the baker had the flour and everything else that goes into good bread. The Barruget wasn't a magician. He was just a good worker.

"That's a splendid idea, my boy," said Creu the builder. "He can get everything we'll need for the road from the gravel pit, and he can use the stuff from there for the road up to your house as well. Why not—you're helping us by letting him work for us. Yes indeed, I've the rocks and the gravel and the cement, all we need."

"Fine then," Tal said. "Early tomorrow I'll tell him to get on with it. Right now Jaime's making him some fish stew, and he does deserve it."

"Oh, he does indeed," said all the fishermen and the men from the farms, and everyone who had seen how the Barruget worked. "He does indeed. And if he comes and helps us, we'll have potatoes and greens and fruit for him."

65

Wwhhhooossh, the Barruget was back. He was grinning from ear to ear as though he'd been having a very good time, and he was blowing himself big and shrinking himself small, turning his ears from blue to green to pink, and bellowing, "WORK OR FOOD!"

"Barruget, well met," said Tal rather fondly. "Look, here's a big pot of fish stew for you."

The Barruget piled into it so fast they hardly saw him chew or swallow. They only saw his huge mouth, opening and closing.

"It's a pleasure to see someone with a good appetite," said one of the fishermen who had stomach trouble.

"It is, that it is," everyone agreed, and stood around fascinated, watching the little monster eat.

When the Barruget began to lick the edges of the pot and make little groaning noises, Tal got up. "Now," he said, "I'd better put him into his bottle."

Chapter Eleven

EVERYBODY heard about Tal's Barruget after that day he helped to bring the big boat on shore at Fishermen's Point. People took special walks to go and look at it, and to see how clean and tidy Tal's and his father's boat was, and they very much admired the paint job on Jaime the fisherman's fishing boat.

When the Barruget took up the building materials for the house on the hill and fixed the road there for Creu the builder, the people were even more impressed.

Not only that, but the bread the Barruget baked was really very good. He kneaded it so thoroughly, the people said to one another. He got the fire going so good and strong. And of course Old Juan the baker was there to take it out at precisely the right moment.

No one really *asked* to have anything done for him, but any time Tal heard of a ditch that had blocked so that water couldn't flow freely into the fields, or of a viaduct that needed emptying and cleaning, or of a rock to be moved when new fishing huts were built into the cliffside of far bays, or when a field had to be cleaned of stones for turning and planting, he'd bicycle down the long red roads with his capacho over his shoulder. Then he'd unsling it, take out the black bottle, pull out the cork, and ask his Barruget to help people who needed that sort of help. And always the Barruget would get a good meal afterward.

Most of the mornings, however, he had the Barruget work at home. They whitewashed their little house inside and out, and painted all the woodwork with the paints they earned by helping Busquet the shopkeeper build a new store. They repaired the garden walls. With Creu the builder's help—he brought the materials—they fixed up not only the little road to their house, but all the others around as well. When Bruja Vieja got her seeds and seedlings they spent a morning planting her vegetable garden. They were going to have all kinds of greens there, not only the usual green peppers, red peppers, tomatoes and potatoes, but also onions and lettuce, chives, cauliflowers, artichokes, cabbages, mint, and all kinds of herbs.

Everything began to show little green shoots almost the minute the Barruget, with Tal watching, and telling him where, had planted them. Of course the weather was also very good that spring.

With Creu the builder's help they fixed up the main street of the village, and all the people brought lovely young trees from their gardens and fincas. The Barruget dug the holes and planted them, *whiz, whooz, whuz,* and every single tree started to flower. The street began to look rather lovely. Then Creu said it would be a good idea to have a better road to San Carlos. So they did that. It took quite a long time because

it's a long road. After that, they fixed up the road to the long lovely beach of Es Cana.

One day as Tal was brushing his teeth out on the terrace and spitting out the toothpaste into a rosebush, he suddenly thought, "I've hardly missed my father at all. I always used to cry when he went away. I wonder why I haven't."

He went into the kitchen where Bruja Vieja was cooking the Barruget's breakfast. (Everybody brought them lots of things for the Barruget to eat. They had no trouble about that at all.) He asked her.

69

"Hmpf," said Bruja Vieja. She looked at Tal. He seemed to have grown at least a couple of inches in the past few months. He was brown and healthy-looking. He was getting too big for his clothes. And his eyes smiled all the time.

"I'll tell you, boy," Bruja Vieja said. "You've been busy working. You haven't had time to be sad. That's the secret, I tell you. You haven't time to think of yourself if you are busy working."

"But I don't think of myself."

"Everybody who is sorry for himself is thinking only of himself," said Bruja Vieja.

"True enough I've been busy," Tal said. "And so has my Barruget. Why, Creu the builder was saying only the other day that Santa Eulalia is getting to be the prettiest little village on the island, with the best roads."

"And our fields are flowering, and our fishing boats go out safe and come back with a good catch, and there is a song in the village." Bruja Vieja sounded as though she were talking to herself.

"Of course," Tal said, "the Barruget couldn't do it alone. You have to give him the idea, and the materials, and then you must be there to tell him what you want done. But I must say he's a willing worker."

" 'Give us the tools,' " said Bruja Vieja, cackling her old cackle, " 'and we shall finish the job.' That's one of the wisest sayings of this rather foolish century. There must be all sorts of people in the world, Tal. The people who realize what has to be done, and the people who are able to supply the things to do it with, and of course, just as importantly, the people to do it."

"I'm not entirely certain I understand what you say," Tal said, "but I do understand what you mean."

So that was the way life went on in Santa Eulalia del Rio, that warm and flowering spring, many years before any tourists came there. The river blew spume over the little cascade under the old bridge, and burbled about things it had seen. Everyone went there to gossip and wash his hair in the clear fresh water. Orchards blossomed and streets were full of flowering trees. Tal bicycled, with his capacho over his shoulder, wherever there was a big job for the Barruget to do, and all the people welcomed them, laughed to see them work, and sang as they helped.

That was how, that spring, Santa Eulalia came to be one of the happiest and prettiest and cleanest little villages on the island.

And as for Tal's little house, it couldn't have been tidier. Tal hardly needed the Barruget to do the cleaning in his own room and his own garden, because after the big jobs they had tackled those seemed such easy things to do himself.

Then, one day when all the flowers were at their best, Tal got a telegram from his father. "COMING HOME TOMORROW. BRINGING YOU A NEW MOTHER FOR YOUR APPROVAL."

Chapter Twelve

TAL TOOK THAT TELEGRAM from his father to the terrace. Already there was quite a lot of shade from the grapevine. Everything grows fast in the Ibizenco spring.

"Well," he said to himself, sitting there with his capacho next to him. "That's that, isn't it."

He wondered how he would like it. Someone new in the house. He didn't remember his own mother, really, because he had been so very young when she died. But he did wonder whether he wanted anyone else coming to his own house. His father and he, after all, had gotten along pretty well.

And then he thought to himself, but I didn't really miss him. Only at night, and in the mornings. And I can get along, whatever.

She'll probably be nice too. He wouldn't like anyone I wouldn't like.

Bruja Vieja's cat, Gato, came and curled up beside him. Absently he stroked her. Then he felt a familiar hand on top of his head. Bruja Vieja was behind him.

"Well, boy, what's it, then?" she asked brusquely.

"Nothing wrong with our spring, was there, Bruja?" Tal said.

"Nothing at all. Busy, true enough. But boys will be boys, and Barrugets are Barrugets."

"There'll be changes now, won't there. Like this lady my father is bringing back to us."

"Never you mind," said Bruja Vieja. "She'll never have seen the likes of us before."

"Do you, do you think she'll like us?"

"She had better, hadn't she." Bruja Vieja cackled. "We know a thing or two, don't we, if she doesn't."

"Oh, we couldn't trouble her," Tal said. "If my father is bringing her, and wants to, we just can't trouble her."

"No one will," the old woman gave Tal an unexpected hug.

"Just you remember, boy," she said "I've never known a better boy across all the centuries, and all the lands. And I know far and well and plenty. She'll find that out, soon enough. Your father wouldn't be picking anyone stupid to bring home. And get off with you, now. I've my bits and pieces to do."

Tal watched her go. She had surprised him. She'd never said such nice things about him before.

Of course he knew she loved him. Often he'd awakened to find her covering him up when the nights were cold, or opening the windows on breathless summer nights. And she was always around, to help him. But she hadn't said much, and he was pleased and surprised. Absently he pulled out the black bottle from his capacho and fiddled with the cork.

Puff, the Barruget was out of it.

74

Tal was about to say that he didn't want anything done right then, nor did he have any food ready, when the Barruget twisted his blue ears with his green hands.

"Young master," he said.

"My name is Tal," Tal said.

"Thank you for your courtesy, Tal," the Barruget said. "I was once called Tomas. A thousand or so years ago, in a cold land of song, where I was accidentally taken in a black bottle."

"I'm glad you are finally speaking to me, Tomas," Tal said. "I've been wondering if we've been working you too hard. And not giving you enough to eat?"

"Not at all, not at all," said Tomas the Barruget. "I've had a splendid time, thank you. But do you know, I'd forgotten all about being alive, for so long."

"What do you mean, alive, Tomas?"

"Well, see, I was asleep in that flower—it must have been for centuries—until you fetched me that night of the right moon and the right bloom. Now I begin to remember."

"What do you remember, Tomas?"

"That is not yet for you to know, young master Tal," said the Barruget. "But remembering, I'd like to return."

"Where will you go? I like having you with me."

"I cannot tell where I will go, for it will be in space and time, and air and sea, and hearts and minds, and dimensions you don't yet know. But I will tell you that you'll always have me with you if you set me free."

"But you *are* free," Tal said, "you are out of the bottle, and you are not bellowing."

"Yes, but you must still say the word."

"If I said the word to get you back into the bottle, would you go?"

"I don't have to, now, because you have spoken to me like an equal spirit, but since you have, I would."

"So if I say you can't go, you won't go?"

The Barruget grew a lot taller. All his colors came on and off. For a minute Tal felt as though he were turning a little green himself, and as though there were only sea and air and timelessness.

They looked at one another for a long serious moment. And then they laughed like good friends.

"Well met, Barruget," Tal said.

"Well met, human boy. Have work and joy," said the Barruget. He turned to go. Then he turned back.

"Are you sure you will let me go?"

76

"Of course," said Tal. "If you want to."

Anyhow, the village was really very neat and tidy now, and Bruja Vieja and he would have to start preparing for the return of his father.

All the same, as Tal looked at the sea far below the flowering orchards, and at the black bottle, quite empty now, he felt just a little sad.

Early next morning Tal woke up because he thought he'd heard the sound of silver bells.

The first thing he saw was the black bottle he had brought up with him, for the last time. After all, without the Barruget there was no point to it any longer.

It was just an old empty bottle.

Yet now, trailing from it, there was a long spray of the strange scented flowers from below the old bridge. Did he hear a sound, a susurrant sound, too? Or was it just the sound of the sea on the shores below?

The flowers stirred as he watched them. Tal thought of Tomas, his Barruget, and thought how lucky he was to have met someone from so far in the past.

Smiling at the memory of the little demon, he said aloud to himself, "*Adios* then, friend Barruget. Well met."

He washed his face and brushed his teeth and put on a clean shirt and clean shorts.

Then he went off to meet his father.

ABOUT THE AUTHOR

EVA-LIS WUORIO was born in Viipuri, an ancient walled Finnish city by the sea. As a child she went to live in Toronto, Canada, in the middle of a vast continent, but the sound and love of the sea never left her. So when she went back to work as a journalist in Europe she made her headquarters on the small Mediterranean island of Ibiza in the Balearics, which is the setting for this story. Her English home at the present time is on the Channel Island of Jersey.

As a feature writer and columnist on newspapers, and as an editor on magazines, Miss Wuorio has traveled by canoe, camel, reindeer, and jet in search of stories. She also writes adult fiction, often espionage and mystery, as well as her charming books for children.

ABOUT THE ARTIST

BETTINA EHRLICH has written and illustrated over fifteen books for children, and has done illustrations for many others. Her beautiful books, many of them with Mediterranean island settings, have been exhibited in London and elsewhere, and she has also won awards for her textile designs. With her husband, a sculptor, she now divides her time between homes in London and in Grado, Italy.